First published in Great Britain in 2017 and in the USA in 2018 by
Otter-Barry Books, Little Orchard,
Burley Gate, Herefordshire, HR1 3QS

www.otterbarrybooks.com

A catalogue record for this book is available from the British Library.

ISBN 978-1-91095-911-4

Illustrations created digitally in Photoshop

Cover lettering by Lottie Burnham

Printed in China

1 3 5 7 9 8 6 4 2

For my best friends,
husband John Avon,
and father
James MacCarthy

Run, Elephant, Run

AN INDONESIAN RAINFOREST ADVENTURE

PATRICIA MacCARTHY

Otter-Barry BOOKS

A storm is coming
to the rainforest.

Rain begins to fall in
diamond drops.
spit spot spit spot

Little Elephant
stays close to his mother.

Wind blows the trees and leaves.
swish sway swish sway
The rain falls faster.
pitter patter pitter patter
Little Elephant is scared.

The wind blows harder and bends the trees.
Heave-ho! Heave-ho!

Rain pelts down.
rattle rattle rattle rattle

An old tree CRACKS and CRASHES
to the ground.

Creatures tumble from its branches
and soon Little Elephant
can't find his mother.

Howling wind **whistles and wails**
whistles and wails.

Rain is **drumming drumming drumming!**

Little Elephant must run for his life.
A tiger is coming his way!

The storm goes wild.
Everything **whirls and swirls,** **whirls and swirls.**

The rain slashes and smashes.
whoosh swoosh **whoosh swoosh**

No time to hide now.
Run, Little Elephant, run!

Faster, FASTER!
Little Elephant
battles against the wind,
the rain and the
slippery mud.

slip-slop slip-slop

LOOK OUT!
The tiger is coming closer!
But Little Elephant slips
and falls. He slides down
a muddy slope on his knees... **whoosh**

FLOP! He bumps straight into his mother!
She has been looking for him everywhere,
and now she holds him close and comforts him.

The elephants **trumpet** loudly, **STAMP** their big feet
and scare the enemy away.
Now it is the tiger's turn to run for his life!

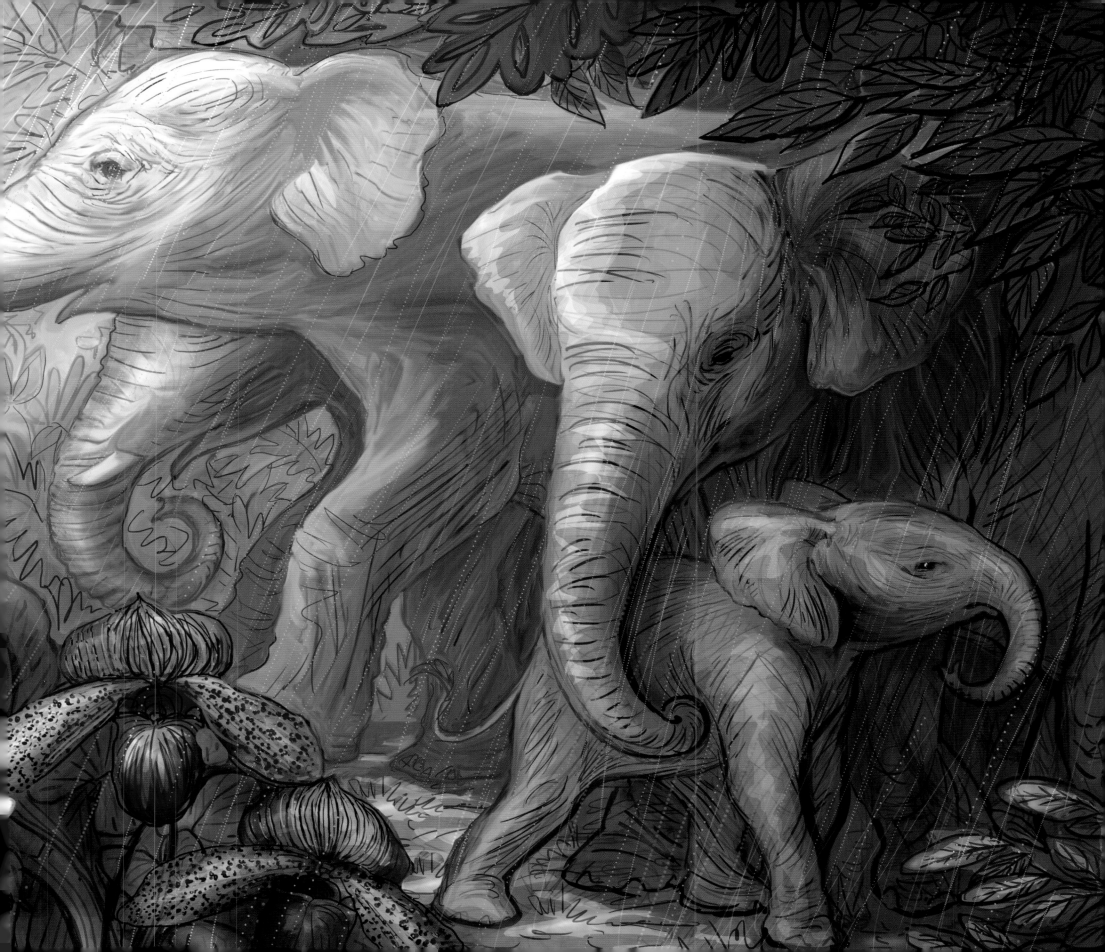

At last the storm is over.
The rain slows to a gentle
pitter-patter spit spot spot spot.

The herd moves on,
and Little Elephant trots
beside his mother.
He has already forgotten
being lost, chased and scared.

But something else has changed too...

Little Elephant feels
BIGGER and **braver**.

He trumpets and stamps his little feet.
STAMP STAMP

Creatures in the canopy call back.

toot toot hoot hoot
The sky is blue, and sunlight
shines into the forest.
Steam rises in the heat.
drip drop drip drop

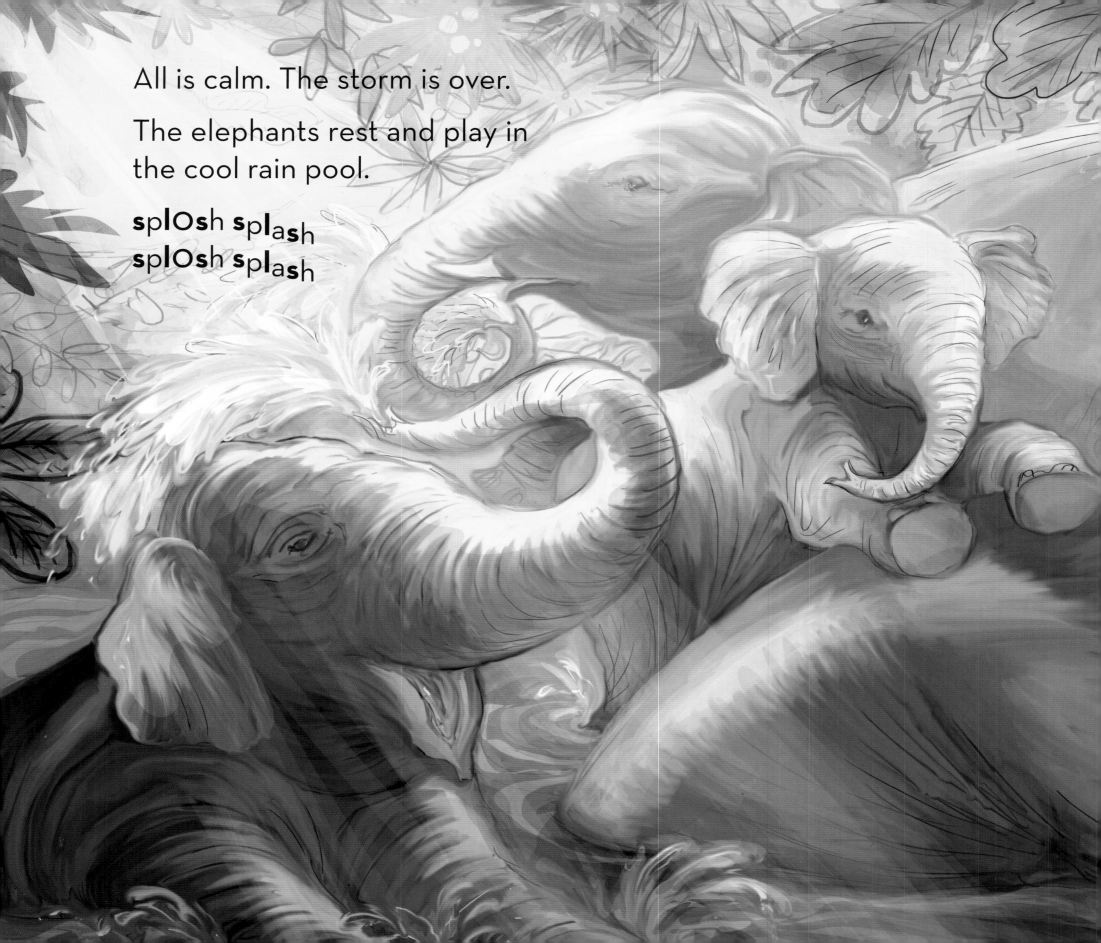

All is calm. The storm is over.

The elephants rest and play in the cool rain pool.

splOsh **spl**a**sh**
splOsh **spl**a**sh**

Little Elephant feels safe and happy again, after his big rainforest adventure.

Can you find these 35 creatures in the book?
They all live in the tropical rainforests of
Indonesia, in South-East Asia.

White-lipped Tree Frog

Asian Elephant

Sulphur-crested Cockatoo

Sunda Sambar Deer

Paper Kite Butterfly

Rhinoceros Hornbill

Siamese Crocodile

Sumatran Tiger

Great Hornbill

Papuan Lorikeet

Orchid Mantis

Long-tailed Macaque

Gray's Leaf Insect

Big-eye Green Whipsnake

Asian Tapir

Pinocchio Tree Frog

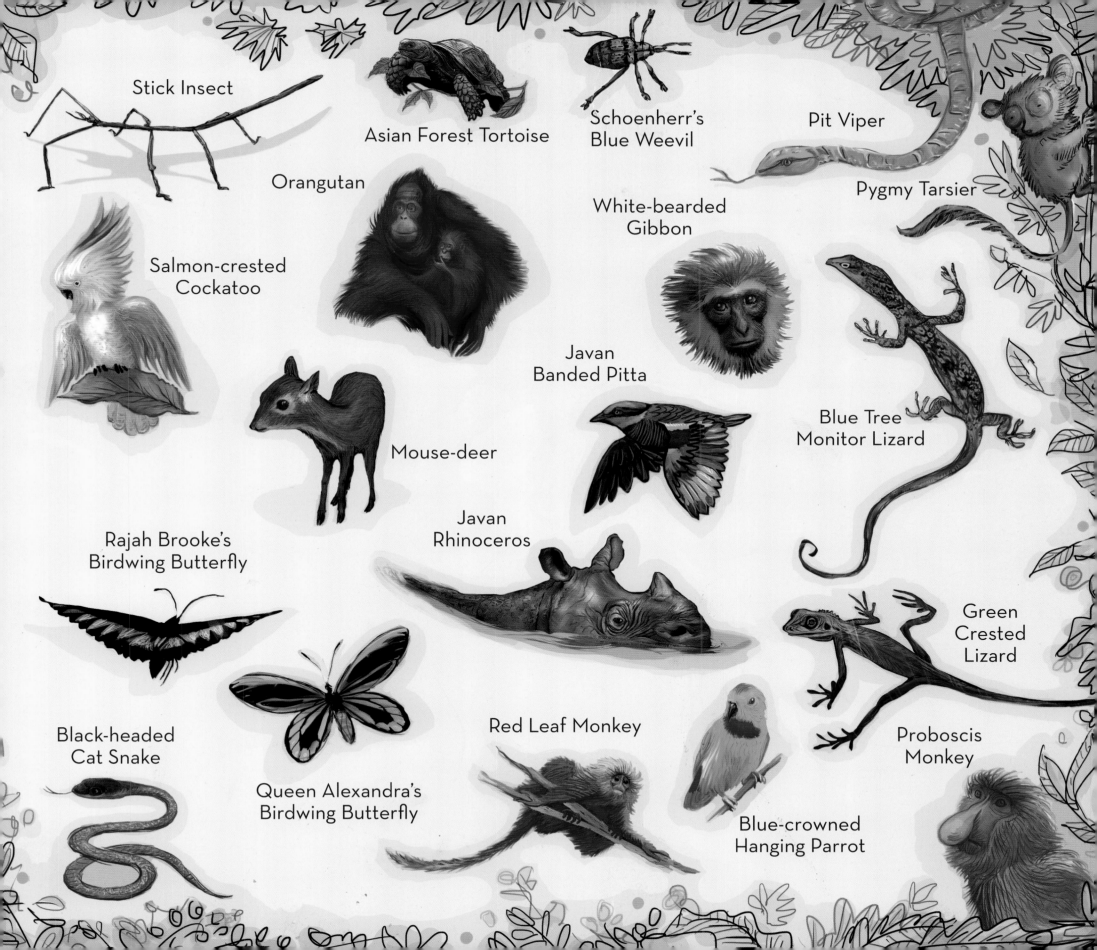

Stick Insect

Asian Forest Tortoise

Schoenherr's
Blue Weevil

Pit Viper

Pygmy Tarsier

Orangutan

White-bearded
Gibbon

Salmon-crested
Cockatoo

Javan
Banded Pitta

Blue Tree
Monitor Lizard

Mouse-deer

Rajah Brooke's
Birdwing Butterfly

Javan
Rhinoceros

Green
Crested
Lizard

Black-headed
Cat Snake

Red Leaf Monkey

Proboscis
Monkey

Queen Alexandra's
Birdwing Butterfly

Blue-crowned
Hanging Parrot